MOST-OF-THE-TIME

MAXIE

MOST-OF-THE-TIME

MAXIE

A STORY BY

ADELAIDE HOLL

PICTURES BY

HILARY KNIGHT

Xerox Family Education Services

XEROX

Maxie was Maxie, most of the time —
  Maxie MacDougal McCoy.
He was not very big, and not very small,
Not very short, and not very tall,
  Just an everyday kind of a boy.

But he had the most marvelous, magical powers.
He could do the most wonderful stunts.

At the drop of a hat—maybe quicker than that—
He could stop being Maxie, at once,

And turn into Terrible Peg-Legged Pete,
A buccaneer dashing and bold,

With a black moustache, and a crimson sash,
And a shipful of pirate gold.

He could turn into Mighty Chief Hawk Eye, the brave,
All painted, and feathered, and fine,

Or a driver named Mack, who whizzed 'round the track
In his racing car Seventy-Nine.

As Tex, he rode off to the roundup in spring,

And he camped on the prairie at night.

As Astronaut Ace, he zoomed into space,
Blasting off on an orbital flight.

He visited Mars and far-distant stars,
Where he saw the most wonderful sights.

Sometimes when he went on a big game hunt,
His name was Sir Anthony Dare.
With his helmet and gun, in the hot jungle sun,

He would track the wild beast to its lair
And capture a gnu to send to the zoo,
Or a lion, or tiger, or bear.

When he fought the wild bull down in Old Mexico,
He was Carlos, the great matador,

And when he was Atlas, The Great Muscle Man,
He could lift sixteen tons — maybe more.

When there was a fire to fight,

Like an arrow he sped in his engine of red

And as daring Sir Gay, he galloped away
In armor all shiny and bright,

Looking brave and defiant, to battle a giant,
And slay every dragon in sight.

When he covered the beat on the big city street,
He was Officer Patrick O'Lear.

As Small Cactus Pete, he would often compete
At riding a wild Texas steer.

In spite of his size, he would win every prize,

And oh, how the people would cheer!

Maxie could do the most wonderful things.
He could walk a high wire with ease.

He could tame savage bears, using nothing but chairs,
  And perform on the flying trapeze.

He could pilot a plane, or a fast diesel train,

Or whiz through the streets in his taxi.
But, quick as a wink, what do you think?

He could change back to just plain Maxie!